MAGIC
FOOTBALL

BY FRANK LAMPARD

FRANKIE'S MAGIC FOOTBALL

TEAM T. REX

FRANK LAMPARD

LITTLE, BROWN BOOKS FOR YOUNG READERS
www.lbkids.co.uk

LITTLE, BROWN BOOKS FOR YOUNG READERS

First published in Great Britain in 2016 by Hodder and Stoughton

1 3 5 7 9 10 8 6 4 2

Copyright © Lamps On Productions Ltd, 2016

The moral rights of the author and illustrator have been asserted.

A CIP catalogue record for this book
is available from the British Library.

ISBN 978-0-349-13211-2

Typeset in Cantarell by M Rules
Printed and bound in Great Britain by
Clays Ltd, St Ives plc

The paper and board used in this book are made
from wood from responsible sources.

MIX
Paper from
responsible sources
FSC
www.fsc.org   FSC® C104740

Little, Brown Books for Young Readers
An imprint of
Hachette Children's Group
Part of Hodder and Stoughton
Carmelite House
50 Victoria Embankment
London EC4Y 0DZ

An Hachette UK Company
www.hachette.co.uk

www.hachettechildrens.co.uk

*To my mum Pat, who encouraged me
to do my homework in between kicking
a ball all around the house, and is still
with me every step of the way.*

*Welcome to a fantastic
Fantasy League – the greatest
football competition ever held
in this world or any other!*

*You'll need four on a team,
so choose carefully. This is a lot
more serious than a game in the
park. You'll never know who your
next opponents will be, or
where you'll face them.*

*So lace up your boots, players,
and good luck! The whistle's
about to blow!*

The Ref

CHAPTER 1

"Just a bit more!" called Louise.

Frankie reached for the next handhold, the muscles in his legs and arms straining. He glanced back over his shoulder at his friends on the ground below.

"You can do it!" said Charlie.

Frankie's fingertips found a small ledge. A trickle of sweat stung his eyes. As he blinked it away, he felt his fingers slip. *No!* But there was nothing he could do. He felt his grip loosen and his body fall away, toppling back from the climbing wall.

Oof! The harness snagged around his waist and jerked him to a halt, mid-air. He dangled on a rope in front of the wall, spinning slightly.

"Not again!" he said.

The instructor let out the rope to lower Frankie down. As soon as his feet touched the floor, Louise came over and gave him a pat on the back. "Never mind," she said. "You're getting closer every time."

Frankie knew she was trying to be kind, but he was really annoyed with himself. He gazed up at the climbing wall. It was about ten metres high and dotted with crevices and bumps and holes, all to help climbers pick their way to the top. It didn't look *that* hard, but Frankie had tried and failed three times in a row.

"You need to relax up there," said the instructor, a young woman with toned muscles. She unclipped Frankie's harness. "If you tense up, it uses energy." She turned to Charlie. "Do you want a turn?"

"Can I keep these on?" asked

Charlie. He held up his hands, showing her the goalie gloves that he always wore.

"You won't get very far if you do," said the teacher. "You won't be able to grip any of the handholds."

"I'll give it a miss, then," said Charlie.

The teacher looked puzzled.

"He's a bit weird about his gloves," Frankie explained, smiling. "He likes to wear them at all times. You know, in case there's a goal to save." It all made perfect sense if you knew Charlie.

"What about you?" the teacher asked Louise.

Louise shrugged. "I don't think I'll be very good at it."

"Nonsense," said the teacher. "Anyone can do it."

"Go on, give it a try," said Frankie.

While they waited for Louise to get the safety harness on, Frankie took off his helmet and glanced around the holiday camp. There were kids splashing in the pool, and he could hear the *pop ... pop ...* of people playing tennis nearby. It was only the second day of their holiday, and he loved it here. They'd already been kite-flying that morning, but there were so many activities to try. He worried they might not manage them all in the week ahead.

However, there was another reason he was excited. A magical reason.

Louise stood ready in her helmet and harness.

"Off you go," said the instructor. "Remember, take your time."

"And don't think about the long drop," added Charlie.

Louise grinned uncertainly as she placed her hands on the climbing wall. She reached out a foot on to a narrow ledge at waist height, then hoisted her weight upwards.

"Good start!" said Frankie.

But the words had barely left his mouth when Louise was up to the next handhold, moving as quickly as a monkey. In hardly any time at all, she was halfway up the wall, her long limbs spread and gripping different areas.

"Wow – she's a natural athlete!" said the instructor. "Does she play other sports?"

"Football!" said Charlie and Frankie together.

Louise continued to climb, her body perfectly balanced, and soon she reached the top of the wall, swinging her leg over and sitting proudly above them. "That was so cool!" she called down.

"Looks really easy to me," said a voice.

Frankie turned to see his older brother Kevin standing behind him, with a sulky look on his face.

The instructor grinned. "Trust me, it isn't. You can try, if you want?" She pointed to a table covered in helmets and ropes.

Kevin blushed. "Ah ... er ... I can't now."

"Why not?" asked Charlie, smirking.

"Because, freckle-features, I've been sent to get you for the barbecue," said Kevin.

"Yum," said Frankie. "Sausages!"

"And burgers!" said Charlie.

"You're making *me* hungry," said the instructor. "Let's get your friend down."

"And Kev can show us how to climb the wall tomorrow," said Charlie.

But Kevin was already stalking off.

*

Frankie could smell the burning charcoal before they reached the cabins. Max ran towards him, tail wagging, and Frankie tickled his chin. Charlie and Louise's parents were sitting on fold-up chairs by a table, while his dad was wafting a barbecue with a newspaper. Flames leapt up over the grill and the aroma of burned meat filled the air. He grinned at Frankie. "Food's nearly done!" he called.

Frankie's mum looked up from her glass of fruit juice. "I think the food might be slightly *over*done," she muttered with a smile.

Frankie laughed. His dad had never been that good at cooking.

There were salads on the table, and bread rolls, and fruit. Frankie poured himself and his friends glasses of orange squash. All that climbing had been thirsty work.

Finally, his dad placed a tray of blackened burgers and sausages in the middle of the table. "*Bon appétit*!" he cried.

Kevin scoffed. "Is that supposed to be dinner? Because it looks like lumps of coal."

Charlie's dad gingerly picked up a sausage and brought it to his mouth. He took a small bite. "No, it's really nice," he said, as his face screwed up. "Honest."

Frankie's dad laughed. "Tell you what, let's order takeaway. Chinese?"

Everyone agreed, and Frankie's mum went inside to order.

Frankie heard Max whine by his ankles. His dog looked up at him with big, sad eyes.

"I know what you want," said Frankie. He threw Max a burned sausage, which Max swallowed in two mouthfuls, looking very pleased with himself.

"Delivery will be half an hour," said Frankie's mum, emerging from their cabin. "We can tuck in to the salad until it arrives."

"Yuck — I hate salad," said Kevin.

Frankie glanced at Louise and Charlie. Louise winked. "We could have a quick game of football," she said.

Frankie knew exactly what she was thinking. She wanted to see what amazing world his magic football would take them to this time. "Great idea," he replied. "I'll get my magic . . ." He checked himself. "I mean, my football."

Soon they were all running to the far side of the holiday camp with

Max at their heels. Signs told them that the theme park was still closed due to an electrical problem, but Frankie ignored them. He had the magic football tucked under his arm, and that meant *anything* was possible. Last time they came here, the football had turned a ride called "Galaxy Quest" into a real space rocket zooming into outer space.

Frankie paused at the gate and peered inside, just in case there were any park staff.

"All clear!" he said.

They snuck through the gate. The theme park was exactly as they'd left it. All the rides were shut down, with no lights, no music and no attendants.

The Galaxy Quest ride was silent. Frankie peered at the other attractions. There was a ghost house, a huge part-deflated bouncy castle and something called "Under the Sea". But his eyes fell on a roller coaster called "T. Rex Runaway". It threaded between fake boulders and volcanoes, and under rainforest trees. Pretend dinosaurs loomed over the track.

He saw Charlie was looking at the same thing. "Let's try that one!" he said.

"Are you sure?" said Louise. "It might be dangerous."

"The football has always kept us safe before," said Frankie.

Louise nodded. They all scrambled into the cart, and pulled down the safety bars. Max sat on Frankie's lap.

Nothing happened.

Frankie looked at the football between his feet. "Oh," he said. "I thought—"

A hissing sound interrupted him and the cart jerked forward. The football sparkled.

"It's working!" said Charlie. "Hang on, everyone!"

CHAPTER 2

Frankie's back pressed against the seat as the cart rattled up the track. Glancing over the edge, it looked much higher than it had seemed on the ground. A ball of nerves was building in his gut. Louise's knuckles were white where they gripped the safety bar. Max had flattened his ears.

They reached the highest point,

and over the wall of the theme park Frankie could see the holiday camp stretching out. He worried for a moment that people might see them, but then the cart began to tip forward slowly.

"Woo-hoo!" yelled Charlie as they plummeted down the other side. Frankie felt the wind dragging against his cheeks. The cart shot down the slope, then leaned to one side as the track entered a turn. It climbed again up a loop, and Frankie lost his bearings as it turned upside down. For a second he was weightless, then they zoomed down the other side.

This is awesome! he thought.

He saw a huge model dinosaur head in front of them, as big as a van. Its mouth gaped, revealing dagger-like teeth. The track went straight through its open jaws and into the dark tunnel beyond. Frankie pushed himself against the seat and they all screamed as the cart headed into the unknown.

But as they entered the darkness, the rattling stopped. It was as if the cart had left the track completely. Frankie felt suddenly weightless. They were mid-air! He saw light ahead — the end of the tunnel. It grew as they flew towards it.

Frankie made out a rocky fringe, and green plants beyond. The cart soared out into the open, then fell towards the ground in some sort of forest.

"We're going to crash!" cried Louise.

Frankie braced himself for impact, but the cart landed with a splash, throwing muddy water over all of them. Bubbles rose from a stinking, oozing marsh as the cart began to sink. If they didn't get out soon ... Frankie looked frantically around. They were only a few metres from the bank.

"Quick – get out!" said Frankie.

He pushed up the safety bars and
took Max under his arm. Louise had
already leapt for the bank. One of
her feet sank up to the knee in the
boggy ground. She tugged it free as
Charlie made the jump too.

Frankie felt the cart wobble
beneath him as it sank deeper into

the marsh. He looked at the jump. It was too far to jump whilst carrying Max and the football. "Here!" he called, as he threw the ball to Louise. She caught it and tucked it beneath her arm.

"Don't you dare throw me," said Max.

"I have to," said Frankie. "Otherwise neither of us will make it."

"I'll catch him," said Charlie, spreading his arms.

"I'm not a football!" said Max.

"Sorry, boy," said Frankie. He steadied himself as the back end of the cart disappeared into the

26

marsh water. It sent up a bubble of gassy air that stank of rotten eggs. Taking careful aim, he hurled Max through the air. His dog whined, legs scrabbling, but Charlie caught him neatly.

"Nice save," said Louise, above Max's yelps of protest.

Frankie climbed into the front of the cart and balanced on the front edge. If he didn't make it the marsh would swallow him up.

One, two ... three!

He swung his arms through the air and launched himself off the cart. His hands reached the bank but both legs slid back into the marsh. He could feel the mud gripping him and panic surged through his veins as he felt his body sink.

Suddenly, a pair of hands reached out to tightly grip his left wrist. He felt another pair of gloved hands grab his right hand. Louise and Charlie braced their feet against the grass and heaved Frankie out of the marsh. He slid on to the muddy bank, breathing hard.

"Thanks," he said.

By the time he turned around, the cart was vanishing beneath the surface of the swamp. That had been too close for comfort.

"Where are we?" asked Charlie.

Frankie climbed to his feet. He tried to ignore the trembling in his limbs. Huge trees towered above them, hanging with thick creepers. He couldn't see the sun, but rays of light pierced the high canopy. Ferns the size of boat-sails cast shadows across the ground. The air was hot and thick like a sauna. But most of all, Frankie noticed the sounds — rustles, chirrups, hoots, and croaks — coming from every direction.

"It's like a rainforest," said Louise.

Frankie heard a buzzing, and

Max barked in alarm. "You don't get those in a rainforest, do you?" said his dog.

Frankie ducked as something swooped close to his head. He saw a massive dragonfly, as big as a seagull, whizz past. Its wings were sparkling turquoise.

"This is a rainforest, but everything's too big. It must be way, way back in the past," said Louise.

"You mean we've gone back in time?" said Charlie.

"It makes sense," said Frankie, marvelling at his surroundings. "The football must have brought us to

prehistoric times! The question is —
why?"

A branch cracked nearby and
they all jumped.

"Maybe we should get moving,"
said Max. "If there are giant
dragonflies, there might be giant
cats too!"

As they walked away from the
marsh, Frankie tried not to think
about the cart. He hoped it wasn't
their only way home. Soon they
were all dripping with sweat. Picking
a path through the undergrowth
was hard. Mammoth tree roots
towered over them as they wound
across the forest floor, and they

had to help each other over. Some of the plants were beautiful but some looked deadly, as if they could swallow you up.

Soon the trees began to thin out, and Frankie and his friends saw a huge cliff face ahead, stretching in both directions. The surface was jagged and covered in plants such as mossy lichen and snaking vines.

They all craned their necks back and stared up at the sheer wall.

"We'll never get up there," said Charlie. "Let's find a way around."

Max suddenly barked. "Hey, check this out!"

Frankie spotted his dog sniffing

around a spiky bush, but there was something balanced in it — something smooth and shiny. Frankie walked over, and saw at once it was an egg. An egg bigger than Max, pale lilac with brown spots.

"What type of creature lays an egg like that?" said Louise.

"A very big hen," said Charlie.

Frankie looked up, squinting. High above, maybe a hundred metres up, he saw the edges of a giant nest on a ledge.

"It must have fallen out of there," he said, pointing. "The bush cushioned its fall."

Max hopped on to his hind legs, and placed his front paws on the eggshell. He sniffed. "Doesn't smell like a hen," he said.

The egg shifted under the weight of Max's body. It rolled off the bush and hit the ground with a *thud.*

"Oops," said Max.

The egg wobbled and a crack opened across its surface. They all jumped back. The split widened, and more cracks spread. Frankie wasn't sure what to do. Should they run?

A piece of eggshell fell away and a dark scaly nose broke through. Then a long head pushed out,

34

shaking from side to side. It made a chirping sound.

"That's no chicken," said Max.

"Oh, it's cute!" said Louise.

The rest of the egg fell apart and a creature sprawled on the fragments. It stood up clumsily on skinny legs, with three blunt little talons at the end of each foot. Frankie gasped as it unfurled huge leathery wings. The creature threw its head back and opened its mouth. Max whined as a roar echoed through the trees. Frankie could feel his hair blown back in a blast of breath.

"It's a ... it's a ..." Frankie had

seen pictures of a creature like this in a book at school. He'd never imagined he'd ever get to see one in real life, and now he was too shocked to speak.

"It's a pterodactyl!" Louise finished for him.

CHAPTER 3

The baby dinosaur's gaze
settled on Max. Frankie's dog
growled, the hair rising along
his spine.

The pterodactyl chirped, cocking
its head.

"Stay back!" said Max. "I'm not
scared of you."

The baby stepped forward,
lowering its head.

"It likes you," said Louise. "It must think you're its mother."

"Very funny," said Max.

"I'm serious," said Louise. "It's called *imprinting.* The first thing a newborn sees, it believes is its parent."

The pterodactyl pressed its snout against Max's neck and made a purring sound. The creature didn't seem quite so scary now.

"Ooh – that tickles," said Max.

"What shall we call it?" said Charlie.

"Er . . . Tommy," said Max.

"How do you know it's a boy?" said Frankie.

"I don't," said Max. "But if I'm his

mum, then I get to name him. It's only fair."

Tommy spread his wings again and flapped. He managed an awkward hop.

"He hasn't learned to fly yet," said Charlie.

"He'll get there," said Max, with a hint of pride.

Frankie looked up at the nest again and frowned. "I think I know why the football brought us here," he said. "We have to get Tommy back to his real mother."

"By teaching him to fly?" asked Louise. "I don't fancy our chances of climbing up—"

The ground trembled, cutting her off. They all looked around.

"What was that?" muttered Charlie.

A further quake shook them, then another. "I don't think it's an earthquake," said Frankie. "It's too regular."

"It sounds like a herd of elephants," said Louise, "but they didn't have elephants in prehistoric times."

The foliage stirred a short distance away as the rumbles closed in. Frankie heard a deep voice.

"I smell something!" it said. "Food."

"You're always hungry," said another voice. "Anyway, it smells horrible."

"That's because you're a vegetarian," said the first voice again. "It's meat. *Fresh* meat."

Frankie's blood ran cold. "I think they're talking about us," he said. "Let's hide!"

Frankie ran to the nearest tree, and cowered in the gap between two huge roots. Louise sheltered behind a drooping fern leaf that reached the ground. Tommy followed close by Max and they scampered behind a boulder at the base of the cliff. Charlie must have found a hiding place, because Frankie couldn't see him when he peered out from his hollow between the roots. Across the clearing, he saw an enormous head push through the leaves of a tree, high up. The head was the size of a car, with two plate-sized yellow eyes, and sharp teeth peeping out over scaly lips.

"A tyrannosaurus rex!" Louise whispered from behind the leaf.

Frankie swallowed. They'd studied dinosaurs at school. Mr Donald had said that the T. rex was the most deadly carnivore ever to walk the Earth.

As the dinosaur emerged,

standing on two powerful hind legs, its nostrils widened and its eyes narrowed.

Two other dinosaurs lumbered out after the T. rex. Frankie recognised them immediately from his schoolbooks. The first was a triceratops, with an armoured head and three horns. The other had jutting plates along its spine – a stegosaurus. With each step, the ground shook.

"This isn't right," hissed Louise. "Those three dinosaurs didn't live on Earth at the same time."

"They didn't talk, either!" said Max.

It must be the football's magic,
thought Frankie. He looked around
for an escape route. He wondered
how fast a T. rex could run. They
hadn't covered that in Mr Donald's
lessons.

The stegosaurus munched on
some leaves sprouting from a low
branch. "Nothing like a refreshing
leaf," it muttered.

"I hate salad," said the T. rex.
Frankie almost smiled. *Just like
Kevin.* The T. rex sniffed again, then
walked slowly towards the tree
where Frankie was hiding. "What *is*
that smell?"

"These leaves are yummy," said

the triceratops. It had joined the stegosaurus.

The T. rex suddenly stopped short of Frankie's tree and turned towards the broken eggshell. "Ah, pterodactyl chick! Where are you, little chick?"

It paced towards the shell.

This might be our best chance to get away, Frankie thought. *While the T. rex is distracted.*

He clicked his fingers to get Louise's attention.

"Where's Charlie?" she mouthed.

Frankie shrugged. Surely his friend would see them if they ran. He used his fingers to mime

running, and pointed away from the
clearing. Louise nodded.

The T. rex lowered its snout
towards half the broken eggshell.
"Wait a minute . . ." it said.

Frankie saw the eggshell
trembling and his heart skipped a
beat. Charlie was hiding beneath it!

CHAPTER 4

The T. rex used the tip of its nose to flip the eggshell over. And there was Charlie, curled in a quivering ball, completely defenceless. Frankie froze with terror, and Charlie stood up slowly on shaky legs.

The stegosaurus let out a yelp.

"What have we got here?" said the T. rex, licking his lips.

"My name's Charlie," said Charlie.

"Your name is lunch," said the T. rex.

"Just keep it away from me," said the stegosaurus. "It looks weird."

"Quiet," said the T. rex. "You're so unadventurous, Steggy. Try something new for a change."

"No thanks," said the stegosaurus. "I have a sensitive stomach."

"Your fur's a funny colour," said the T. rex. Charlie was wearing a red checked shirt and Bermuda shorts.

"I'm really not very tasty," said Charlie.

Frankie needed to create a distraction. But how could he distract a massive dinosaur?

The T. rex leaned closer to Charlie. "And why are your hands so leathery?"

Charlie backed away, gloves over his face. "Urgh – your breath stinks!"

"We're always telling him that," said the triceratops. "It's the diet – all that meat, and not enough greens!"

The T. rex rumbled with annoyance. "You won't have to smell it for long, little thing."

Frankie's hands tightened on

the magic football. *Of course – a distraction.*

"Ready to be eaten?" said the T. rex.

Charlie paled. "I'm ... always ... ready," he said. Though he didn't look ready at all.

I have to stop this! Frankie thought.

As the T. rex opened its mouth wide, drool spilled over its fangs. Frankie stepped out from his hiding place and threw the ball in the air. Then he blasted it with his right foot, straight across the clearing. *Bam!* It hit the T. rex on the nose. The dinosaur bellowed and backed

away, waving its head in pain.
Charlie snatched the ball as it fell
and ran towards Frankie.

"Let's get out of here!" he cried.

They all fled from the clearing.
Frankie ran like never before. He
imagined he was being chased
along the wing by the fastest
midfielder on the pitch. Max's
paws were a blur and Tommy kept
leaping up into the air, trying to fly
and falling back to the ground. He
let out desperate squeaks.

They ran until the breath in
Frankie's lungs was like fire.
Eventually they stopped, bent
over double and panting. Frankie

strained his ears, but he couldn't
hear any of the dinosaurs following.

"You saved me," said Charlie. "I
thought I was dino dinner."

"No problem," said Frankie.
"You'd have done the same for me."

"This place is going to be full of
things that want to eat us," said
Louise. "The sooner we get Tommy
back to his nest, the better."

Frankie gazed up the cliff. It
wasn't quite as steep here, but it
still looked treacherous. *Somehow
we have to get up there.* His glance
fell on some creepers snaking
across the ground. "Let's use those
as ropes," he said. "If we get into

trouble, we can tie them around our waists and fix them to the cliffs as we go."

"Good thinking," said Louise. "But what about the football? You won't be able to carry it and climb."

Frankie chewed his lip. Louise was right. There was a crack at the bottom of the cliff face and he shoved the ball inside. He didn't like leaving it, but there wasn't much choice. "At least it'll be out of sight," he said.

They broke off the creepers and wound them into coils. The going wasn't too hard at first, more of a steep walk than a climb, so they didn't need the ropes. The rock under their feet was covered in gouges and small bristly plants. They weren't like anything that Frankie had seen before. Tommy skipped up the slope ahead with Max, still flexing his wings and flying a few metres at a time. As they rose above the trees, a light breeze cooled the sweat on Frankie's brow.

He looked back as they reached a plateau. A carpet of thick green vegetation stretched all the way to the horizon. In the distance, mountains smoked.

"Volcanoes!" he said, pointing. The others stopped and stared.

Frankie crouched and laid a hand on the ground. It felt slightly warm. "I think this might be a volcano, too," he said.

Louise stooped down to feel, and Charlie even took off his gloves for a moment.

"I don't like the sound of that," he said, standing up again. "What if it erupts?"

As he finished speaking, the ground rumbled beneath their feet.

"You were saying?" said Max, with a whine.

"Just a little tremor," said Louise. "Nothing to worry ..."

Another quake shook them.

Frankie struggled to stay on his feet.

"That one was harder!" he said.

Then the whole ground lurched up, and they were tipped over. Frankie flung out his hands to break his fall. His stomach flipped as the world seemed to fall away on each side. They were being lifted higher. The ground flexed but didn't break apart like normal rock. A hundred metres away, a blunt head rose on a long neck.

Frankie looked again at the bristling plants at his feet, and the cracks in the grey stone. Only now he realised they weren't plants, and what he was kneeling on wasn't stone at all. They were bristles, and beneath him was ... skin! He gazed around in astonishment. They were standing on a dinosaur's back. The biggest dinosaur ever to walk the Earth.

"It's a diplodocus!" he cried.

CHAPTER 5

The massive dinosaur opened its
mouth in a yawn, and the sound
of a thousand trumpets battered
Frankie's ears.

The diplodocus didn't even seem
to have noticed them. *We're like fleas
on a dog's back,* thought Frankie.

The dinosaur stretched its neck
upwards. At first Frankie thought
it was reaching for the pterodactyl

nest, but it fastened its lips over a bright red plant growing a few metres below and began to chew slowly.

The giant creature took a step, and Frankie clutched his friends close as its back lurched. The dinosaur smashed its side against the cliff face and began to rub back and forth. Clouds of rock and dust rained down.

"It's scratching itself!" said Charlie.

"I think we've hitched far enough," said Frankie. He saw a ledge on the cliff face, just big enough to hold them. "That way!"

With wobbling steps, they crept along the diplodocus's back. They could jump off on to the ledge, but they'd have to time it right. If they didn't make it to the ledge, it was a long drop.

"Get ready!" said Frankie. He grabbed Louise's hand and Charlie's. "Now!" he said.

They leapt together and landed on the ledge just as the dinosaur moved away from the rocks. Max and Tommy made it too.

Frankie stared upwards. Thanks to the ride they'd hitched, it wasn't far to the nest. But it was very steep.

"OK, Louise and I will make the climb," said Frankie. "Then we'll use the creepers to hoist Tommy after us."

"What about me?" asked Charlie.

"You'll have stay here to tie Tommy up," said Frankie.

"Are you sure about this?" asked Louise. "It's pretty dangerous."

Frankie pushed his fear down into his stomach. He remembered how he'd fallen three times on the climbing wall, but Charlie hadn't had any climbing practice at all. "It's the only way. It'll need two of us to pull Tommy up."

"OK," said Louise. "But I'll go first."

She began to climb, with a coil of creeper looped over her shoulder and under her arm. She glanced down when she'd gone a few metres. "Just remember – don't rush."

Frankie reached for a handhold and set off after his friend. He tried to follow her route exactly, placing his fingers and feet in the same spots. But Louise was more flexible – she could bend her body into better positions. Soon Frankie realised he couldn't see the next place to reach for. A gust of wind

buffeted the cliff face and panic spiked in his chest.

Louise had already reached the ledge above.

"I'm stuck!" said Frankie. His arms began to shake with the strain of holding on. He'd have to go back down. But as he looked over his shoulder, a wave of dizziness passed over him. As he moved his right foot, a section of rock broke away under his left. For a moment he dangled in mid-air, holding on to the cliff edge by his fingertips. It felt as though his arms were about to be pulled out of their sockets! The rocks fell and shattered on the ground. Below them, Charlie gave a gasp of shock. Frankie squeezed his eyes tight shut. *I can't do this!*

"Frankie, listen to me," called Louise. "There's a ledge to your right. Move your right foot up a bit."

Frankie forced his eyes open. His whole body was trembling now, but Louise was right. He saw a lip of rock to one side and shifted his right foot over, until – there! He felt solid rock beneath his toes. His heartbeat began to slow.

"Now bend your left knee up to your chest," said Louise. "You can put it on another ledge there."

Again, Frankie found the spot she was talking about. He used his legs to push himself upwards.

"Nearly there," said Louise. "You need to let go with your right hand and reach straight up."

Frankie couldn't. He didn't have a rope to save him this time. If he fell, that was it.

"Trust me," said Louise calmly.

Something about her voice got through the wall of fear. Frankie released the rock with his fingers and reached up. He felt Louise's fingers around his wrist, then heard her grunt as she heaved him to safety. He flopped down beside

her. "Easy peasy, see?" she said
with a grin.

"Something like that," said
Frankie. He was relieved to see the
nest a few metres away, slightly
above them along a rocky path.
It was perched on the cliff edge.
"Let's get Tommy up here."

They unfurled the creeper. Louise
and Frankie watched as, down
below, Charlie fashioned a loop
under Tommy's wings. Then he gave
them a thumbs up. But the baby
pterodactyl let out a keening cry,
wriggling in the lasso. He strained his
body towards Max, almost tugging
Louise and Frankie off the cliff face.

"He doesn't want to leave," said Louise.

"It's all right," said Max, his voice carrying up to Frankie. He laid a paw on Tommy's side. "You'll be with your real family soon."

Tommy gave another chirp, quieter this time. Frankie and Louise braced themselves and heaved, hoisting the baby dinosaur up a little. "And again!" said Frankie. They leaned forward, grabbing the vine further up, and pulled once more. In small stages, they managed to haul Tommy up towards their ledge. Frankie pointed to the nest.

"Time to go home," he said.

Tommy didn't budge. He looked back down to Max.

"Come on," Louise said. "This way." She gave the creeper a light tug like a lead, and they led Tommy over.

This was the first time Frankie had ever seen a dinosaur's nest! It was just like a bird's nest, but as big as a paddling pool. It was made of branches woven loosely together and lined with bits of fur and plants. As Frankie peered over the top, he got a shock. There, among pieces of broken shell, were two other young pterodactyls. They began to squawk in panic and flap their wings when they saw Frankie and Louise.

Tommy hopped in among his siblings. The babies' squawks softened into chirrups of pleasure as they tussled with each other, welcoming him back. All three of them seemed to have forgotten

that Frankie and Louise were even there.

"Thank goodness for that," said Louise. "He seems to know he's home."

Frankie felt his face flush with pleasure. "We did it!"

A piercing screech broke his mood and a shadow passed over him, cooling his skin.

Overhead swooped a giant pterodactyl. It was the size of a small aeroplane, its long bill at least two metres long and leathery wings almost transparent beneath the sun's rays, criss-crossed with slender bones.

"I guess that's Tommy's mum," said Louise.

The mother pterodactyl turned its head towards them and screeched again angrily.

"Are pterodactyls vegetarian?" asked Frankie, as fear tickled his spine. Then he noticed that there were several gnawed bones lying in the nest.

Louise looked at him grimly. "I'm afraid not," she said.

The giant flying dinosaur tipped its wings and dove straight towards them, razor-sharp talons outstretched.

CHAPTER 6

Frankie and Louise ducked as
the massive shape whooshed
overhead. Frankie felt the talons
rip through the back of his T-shirt.
That was too close for comfort!
The baby pterodactyls squealed
in fear as their mother rose again
into the sky. "She doesn't want us
here," said Louise. "We need to
escape."

Frankie didn't see how. The only way down was to climb and, if they did, they'd be exposed on the rock face.

"Are you OK?" called Charlie's voice from below.

"Not really!" shouted Frankie. "We're trapped up here."

He watched the mother pterodactyl circling.

"Leave it with me," said Charlie. "I have a plan!"

I hope it's a good one, thought Frankie. He peered over the edge of the cliff and saw Charlie was scrambling along the ledge beneath. He was reaching for something out of sight, and the rocks were crumbling at his feet.

"Uh-oh," said Louise, as Frankie felt a cold breeze ruffle his hair. "Here she comes again."

The pterodactyl glided down, and landed a few metres from the nest's edge, then folded her massive wings. Frankie gasped. Her bill was lined with hundreds of serrated teeth. She began to stalk closer.

"Charlie, how's that plan coming along?" yelled Louise.

Frankie looked down once more. Charlie had a handful of the red leaves that were growing from the rock face. He was waving them madly.

"I don't think the pterodactyl's interested," said Max.

"It's not for her!" said Charlie. "It's for *him*."

Frankie's glance followed where his friend was pointing. There! The diplodocus lumbered towards the red leaves that Charlie was holding out. His friend had tempted the giant dinosaur back! Frankie still couldn't work out Charlie's plan, though.

Louise grabbed Frankie's arm and pulled him back further into the nest. The mother pterodactyl was just a few metres away. Her eyes gleamed with anger.

"You have to jump!" called Charlie. "On to the diplodocus – any moment now it will be right below the nest."

The pterodactyl stabbed with her beak and Frankie backed away until he was right against the nest's edge. There was nowhere else to go. Tommy was hopping back and forth, obviously distressed, but his mother wasn't paying any attention. All she wanted to do was protect her babies.

"We don't have a choice," said Louise. "We jump together!"

Frankie nodded, scrambling up to the nest's edge with his friend. He saw the diplodocus below, head reaching up for the leaves in Charlie's hands. It was at least five metres down. *I can't be frightened now*, he told himself. *We jump together, or not at all.* He thought back to all the matches they'd played together. He and Louise were a team.

"After three!" he said. "One ... two ..."

The pterodactyl's fierce beak made a grab for them, and with a *yank!* Louise pulled Frankie out over the drop.

They fell like stones. Frankie flexed his knees as he landed on the diplodocus's head. It grunted in surprise, but carried on chewing the leaves Charlie had given it.

"Hop on!" said Louise.

Charlie and Max came right to the edge. Max jumped off the ledge and landed neatly, but the dinosaur moved slightly as Charlie leapt. One foot slipped, and he would have fallen if Frankie hadn't grabbed his arm.

"Thanks!" said Charlie.

Frankie stared along the long neck. "OK, stay close everyone."

They linked hands, and Frankie

led the way down the neck. It was
about ten metres wide, but it felt
like walking along a knife-edge.
If the dinosaur made any sudden
moves, they would all tumble to
their deaths.

They made it to the broad back,
then ran along to the tail. This was

narrow too, but by now the ground was much closer. Frankie slid on his bottom to the tip, then dropped to the ground.

"That was kind of fun!" said Charlie, landing beside him.

Max looked back towards the nest, where they could see the mother pterodactyl squatting protectively over her young.

"I'll miss Tommy," the dog said.

"Me too," said Louise. "But I've had enough of dino world. I say we get back to the swamp and find a way home."

"Yes," said Frankie. "Let's get the football on the way. We've done what it brought us here to do."

He was glad to find the football where he'd hidden it. Using Max's nose to guide them, they set off through the dense foliage. Frankie remembered the cart sinking into the swamp, and hoped the football's magic was strong enough to get them back to the holiday camp. They'd been lucky so far, but he didn't fancy their chances of surviving a night here.

At the swamp's edge, the ball was tingling a little under his arm, like it always did when it was about to work its magic.

"Get ready everyone," he said. He laid the ball on the floor, when he felt the ground vibrate.

"Forgetting something?" said a low, rumbling voice.

The T. rex stomped into the clearing. Its two dinosaur friends came either side.

Charlie sighed. "Look, we haven't got time for a game of football," he said.

"Who said anything about a game?" said the T. rex. "I'm still hungry. Who's the starter? Maybe the four-legged one ..." It lifted a foot and pinned Max's tail to the ground.

Frankie thought fast. "No, take me! He's really stringy."

"Excuse me?" said Max.

"Not even a pedigree!" Charlie added.

The T. rex looked down at Max, then up at Frankie. "You're probably right. All that hair will give me indigestion."

It lifted its foot off Max, who dashed away. The T. rex slowly advanced on Frankie. It was completely blocking the path to the marsh, like the biggest goalkeeper ever. But Frankie saw a gap, right between the T. rex's legs. It was a basic goalkeeping

error – one Charlie never would have made.

As the T. rex stomped closer, Frankie side-footed the ball. It shot low along the ground and landed in the edge of the swamp. Straight away, a shimmering portal opened above the filthy water.

"Go!" said Frankie.

Louise looked at him in terror. "We can't leave you!"

"I'll catch up," said Frankie. "Now run!"

CHAPTER 7

Charlie grabbed Louise's arm and pulled her towards the portal.

"Stop them!" said the T. rex.

The stegosaurus and triceratops charged at Charlie and Louise. But Louise was quicker. She and Charlie jumped hand-in-hand and vanished through the portal. The two dinosaurs collided in a headlong rush and fell into the swamp, throwing up an enormous muddy wave. They came up again, dripping in slime.

"Leaf-munching idiots!" said the T. rex.

With the T. rex distracted, Frankie ran between its legs. The portal was only ten metres away. Max sprinted at his side. Five metres. Frankie got ready to jump . . .

Something huge swiped at him from one side. Just as he realised it was the tip of a scaly tail, the wind was knocked out of him and he sprawled across the ground.

He rolled over and saw the T.

rex's huge foot coming straight down towards him.

The T. rex pinned him to the ground. Frankie stared up between two clawed toes.

Frankie struggled helplessly, but couldn't free himself.

Then he saw something in the sky. Three dots. He wasn't sure what they were, but they were getting closer.

"Any last words?" asked the T. rex.

Frankie squinted as the shapes flew nearer. "Tommy!" he said.

The T. rex frowned. "Who's Tommy?"

The three pterodactyl chicks soared down on their wings. Two landed on the T. rex's back and Tommy landed on its snout.

The T. rex roared in pain as Tommy dug in with his talons. It shook its head wildly and the foot holding Frankie lifted. Frankie rolled quickly out of the way. Screeches and shrieks filled the air as the T. rex staggered back and forth. Its little forearms flailed and its tail thumped the ground as it tried to throw off the winged attackers.

"Thanks, Tommy!" said Frankie. He ran towards the portal, then waited for Max to catch up.

"I'm proud of him!" said Max, looking back at the fight.

"Come on," said Frankie. He picked up his dog and jumped into the portal.

For a moment everything was dark, then Frankie felt something beneath him. A seat. He heard the rattle of the track, felt the wind in his face. Finally, the hiss of brakes.

He found himself sitting in the cart as it rolled to the end of the dinosaur ride. Max sat at his feet, paws on the football. Louise and Charlie were in the cart in front.

"We thought you'd never make it!" said Louise.

"It was a close call," said Frankie.

He climbed out, slightly shaky on his feet. From the position of the sun in the sky, it didn't look like much time had passed at all. Then, through the gates, they saw a van drive past. It had "Wong's Chinese" written on the side.

"That's our dinner!" said Charlie.

They ran back to the cabins, where Frankie's mum was spooning out noodles. "Just in time!" she said.

Frankie sat down and reached over for a set of chopsticks.

"Oh my!" said Charlie's dad. "What happened to your shirt, Frankie?"

Frankie didn't know what he was talking about. "What do you mean?"

The other parents gathered to look. "There's a huge tear across the back!" said his mum.

Frankie went red. He remembered the mother

pterodactyl's talons, up in the nest.
He didn't know what to say.

"Must've got caught on a tree!"
said Louise.

"What were you doing up a
tree?" asked Frankie's mum. "I
thought you were playing football."

"The ball got stuck," Charlie
interrupted. "You know Lou's shots.
All over the place!"

Louise gave him a playful punch
on the arm.

"Sounds like an eventful game,"
said her dad.

"Oh, yes," said Frankie. "It was a
roaring success!"

ACKNOWLEDGEMENTS

Many thanks to everyone at Hachette Children's Group; Neil Blair, Zoe King, Daniel Teweles and all at The Blair Partnership; Luella Wright for bringing my characters to life; special thanks to Michael Ford for all his wisdom and patience; and to Steve Kutner for being a great friend and for all his help and guidance, not just with the book but with everything.

Turn the page for
an exclusive extract
from Frankie's
next adventure,
Deep Sea Dive,
coming soon!

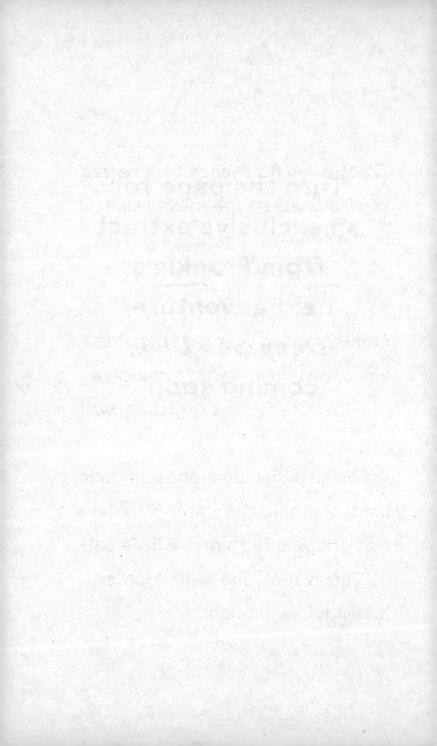

Frankie and his friends have rented rowing boats on the rowing lake at the holiday camp, but Kevin is causing trouble ...

Frankie looked over the side of the boat. The water was too murky to see how deep it was. *Probably not very,* he told himself.

Louise pulled up alongside their boat, churning the water. Charlie was gripping the sides, a little pale.

"This is fun!" she said. "Harder than it looks, though."

Kevin suddenly reached across and grabbed the oars from Frankie.

"Hey!" said Frankie.

Before he could take them back, Kevin began to slap the paddles in the water, throwing waves at Louise's boat. One splashed Charlie, soaking him.

"That's not funny!" he said.

Frankie sighed. He wished they'd never brought Kevin with them.

His brother was laughing as he continued to splash the others, but Louise just sank the oars again, and rowed away.

"Great! Let's race!" said Kevin.

With a lot of rocking, he

managed to turn the boat around.

"Maybe we should just go back to shore," said Frankie.

Kevin began to thrash the oars as he tried to row. He wasn't very good, but soon they were veering in an uneven course after Louise. Max whined between Frankie's feet.

Kevin looked back over his shoulder, keeping on track. Frankie saw that Louise had already reached the line of buoys, and she was making a slow, graceful turn.

"Kev, slow down," said Frankie. "We're heading right for them."

His brother grinned. "I know."

He rowed harder, picking up speed.

Charlie saw them coming. "Stop!" he cried.

Frankie stood up to try and grab the oars from his brother, but it was too late.

Louise's boat was side-on when the boats crashed together with a thump. Frankie saw it wobble and Charlie wailed as water sloshed over the side. Max barked. Thankfully the boat didn't capsize.

"That was stupid!" said Louise angrily.

"Just having a bit of a laugh," said Kevin.

"No one thinks it's funny," said Frankie.

Frankie noticed that both boats had drifted past the buoys and into water that was thick with weeds. Fallen logs and other debris floated on the surface. Tree branches hung over the water like spindly fingers. Looking beyond to the far bank, Frankie realised they were close to the abandoned theme park. He could see the T. Rex Runaway train ride peeping through the trees.

"Let's get back to the proper lake," he said, taking hold of the oars.

"What's wrong with all of you,"

said Kevin sulkily. "Anyone would think you'd never broken a rule before, but I know what you've been up to." He reached with his foot and rolled the magic football out from under the bench, then stood up. "You've been sneaking into that theme park with this."

He tossed the ball in the air, then started to do keepie-uppies. The boat wobbled from side to side.

"Kev, that's enough!" said Frankie. "Give it back."

"Not until you tell me what's been going on," said Kevin. He kicked the ball high and bent down to try and catch it behind his head. It was a hard enough trick on solid ground and he misjudged it. The ball bounced off the back of his head and splashed into the water a few metres away.

"Nice one!" said Charlie.

Frankie reached out with an oar to scoop up the ball, but saw it wasn't there.

"Where's it gone?" he said, with rising panic.

"Maybe it sank," said Kevin.

"It shouldn't do," said Louise.

The water began to swirl on the surface where the ball had fallen in.

"Uh-oh," said Charlie.

The swirl expanded, spinning quicker and quicker, and in its centre the water dropped as if it was being sucked down a plug-hole. Frankie felt his boat start to drift towards it.

"Quick! Row away!" said Kevin.

Frankie did as he said, plunging the oars into the water. Louise was doing the same.

But it was no use. The whirlpool grew, and so did its power. It was pulling them in. Max whined and laid a paw across his eyes.

Kevin and Charlie paddled furiously with their hands, scooping up water.

"What's happening?" yelled Kevin, his face twisted with fear.

"It's the magic football!" said Frankie. "Hold on, everyone."

But Kevin must have seen his chance. As the boat's nose dipped into the whirlpool, he jumped clear, grabbing at a branch that was growing over the water. Frankie saw his brother's legs dangling, and then the world lurched over. He tumbled out of the boat.

Competition Time

COULD YOU BE A WINNER LIKE FRANKIE?

Every month one lucky fan will win an exclusive
Frankie's Magic Football goodie bag! Here's how to enter:

Every **Frankie's Magic Football** book
features different animals. Go to:
www.frankiesmagicfootball.co.uk/competitions
and name three different animals that feature in three
different **Frankie's Magic Football** books.
Then you could be a winner!

You can also send your entry by post by filling in
the form on the opposite page.

Once complete, please send your entries to:

Frankie's Magic Football Competition
Hachette Children's Books, Carmelite House,
50 Victoria Embankment,
London, EC4Y 0DZ

GOOD LUCK!

Competition Entry Page

Please enter your details below:

1. Name of Frankie Book: ....
   Animal: ....

2. Name of Frankie Book: ....
   Animal: ....

3. Name of Frankie Book: ....
   Animal: ....

My name is: ....

My date of birth is: ....

Email address: ....

Address 1: ....

Address 2: ....

Address 3: ....

County: ....

Post Code: ....

Parent/Guardian signature: ....

FRANKIE'S MAGIC FOOTBALL
WEBSITE

Have you had a chance to check out
frankiesmagicfootball.co.uk yet?

Get involved in **competitions**, find out **news** and
updates about the series, play **games** and watch
videos featuring the author, **Frank Lampard!**

Visit the site to join
Frankie's FC today!